To:

HAPPY HALLOWEEN

FROM· EMMANUEL EPISCOPAL
CHURCH

To my biggest supporters of
whatever I do in life,
a.k.a
The Knebel Team!

BACK TO THE PAST

THE KENTS' QUEST #3

by C. Knebel
Simple Words Books™

FREE DECODABLE
PHONICS WORKBOOK
and
FREE ACCESS TO ONLINE SUMMITS

simplewordsbooks.com

Chapter 1
Plans For The Fall

It was last fall when Kim and Tim Kent went to Camp Split Rock with their mom and dad. Back then, Kim was six and Tim was ten.

The trip was such a blast with so much fun stuff to do. They got to help a fox cub get back to his mom and dad.

Plus, they got to track down a bad man and flush out a big pet scam. With their help, the cops got the bad man.

What can top that?

Not the trip this fall!

This fall, the Kents will not go to Camp Split Rock at all. Tim and Kim

will have to spend their days at Camp
Diggin. They will, in fact, dig in the
sand and mud. They will dig for fossils.

Until this fall, there were no kids
at Camp Diggin. It was just the staff.
But last spring, Mr. Prill, who runs
the camp, had a plan to branch out his
camp to kids. He thinks this can bring
him lots of cash and get him out of a
mess with the bank.

When Mr. Prill runs into Mr. and
Mrs. Kent at a brunch, he tells them
that Kim and Tim may like Camp
Diggin.

Mr. and Mrs. Kent think this may
be fun for the kids. They tell Mr. Prill
that they will check with Kim and Tim.
If the kids wish to go, they will contact
him.

The next day, Mr. and Mrs. Kent ask Kim and Tim if they want to go to Camp Diggin in the fall.

The kids do not just say yes, they jump up and down. Digging for fossils! That will be EPIC!

Mr. and Mrs. Kent tell Mr. Prill that the kids are glad to go to Camp Diggin.

Chapter 2
Stuck With Camp Diggin

With just a day until the trip to Camp Diggin, it all sinks in for Tim and Kim.

This is not what they want to do at all. Plus, their mom and dad will not be with them.

So the kids do not want to go to this camp.

Kim tells her mom and dad that she wants to stay with them and their pup, Bud.

Her dad tells Kim that the plan is for her to go to this camp with Tim. Mr. and Mrs. Kent will be on a trip as well. But not with the kids.

"Can Bud be at the camp with us?" Kim asks her mom.

Kim thinks Bud will have fun digging for fossils.

"Bud cannot be at the camp. This is just for kids, no pets," Mrs. Kent tells Kim. "They will not let a pup dig for fossils."

"But Bud is the best at digging," Kim insists.

"I bet the camp staff does not want pups to snack on the fossils," Mr. Kent grins.

"Did you ask them? I think he will do well," Kim nags.

"Bud will be at Pup Inn. That will be fun for him, just like Camp Diggin will be fun for you," Mr. Kent tells Kim.

"There will be lots of kids there to hang out with."

"I will not pack for the camp! If Bud cannot go with me, I will not go," Kim grunts.

Kim's mom and dad get strict.

"You cannot just quit like this on the last day, Kim," says her mom.

"We got the bus tickets for you as well," adds her dad. "You have to go. Just do the best you can to have fun."

The trip is all set. It is just what it is.

There is no backup plan. Mom and Dad will be on a trip to NYC. Bud will be at Pup Inn. And the kids must be at Camp Diggin.

There is no way out.

Kim does not like this a bit. But she gets that they cannot call it off with just a day left until the camp.

Tim thinks Camp Diggin may not be all that bad. It may be fun to dig out a fossil. Yet he still does not want to go. But he does not say a thing to his mom and dad.

The kids will have to spend six days digging for fossils.

There will be no Mom. There will be no Dad. Just Kim and Tim. That is the end of it.

And just like that, Kim and Tim are off to camp.

Chapter 3
At Camp Diggin

The bus trip to Camp Diggin is a drag. Tim expects lots of kids on the bus. But it is just Kim and Tim. They think this is odd.

When they get to the camp, it is hot and damp. There is dust in the wind. It is as if they are in the Old West.

The bus stops on a flat lot in front of a big log cabin. The cabin is a run-down ranch. In front of the cabin is a flag with a T-Rex print on it.

Next to the log cabin are stalls with stacks of hay. To the left of the stalls, there is a hut. Past the hut, there are plots with pits.

Is this where they will dig for fossils?

Mr. Prill is up front with a big grin. He is a big old man with a red top and black pants.

"Who do we have on this bus?" he asks as he grabs the kids' hands and stamps them with a T-Rex print in black ink.

"You must be Tim and Kim," he says.

The kids nod.

"I am Mr. Prill. I run Camp Diggin," he adds.

Then he lifts his hand to the flag with the T-Rex.

"T-Rex is our mascot," he adds. "Do you like it?"

The kids shrug.

"Where are the rest of the kids?" Tim asks.

"What kids?" asks Mr. Prill. "It is just you and Kim with us this fall."

He pats Tim on the back.

"We sent the camp ads to a lot of kids, but we had no luck," he adds. "We are glad to have you with us at the camp for the next six days! We will have lots of fun."

Kim squints back at the bus.

Can she jump back on it if she is quick?

Chapter 4
The Check In

"Six days will go by fast," Tim says to Kim as if he can tell what she thinks.

Mr. Prill helps Tim and Kim with their bags.

"Let us go to my hut!" He claps his hands. "We must check you in. Then we will get you set up for the dig. Chop! Chop!"

Mr. Prill's hut is big and rustic. It does not smell fresh.

In the hut, Mr. Prill has a desk, a bench and a bed. There are a lot of contracts on his desk. It is a big mess.

A big, tall mock-up of a T-Rex stands next to the desk. There is a shelf on the wall with lots of rocks. Next to the rocks is a stack of skulls and shells.

"This is my hut. I spend my days in this hut or out in the plots," Mr. Prill says.

He lifts up a box. The tag on the box says, "Camp Stuff – For Kids."

He brings out red tops and flaps them. The left pocket has the camp mascot T-Rex. They are just like what Mr. Prill has on.

"Kids, this is what the staff and I dress in. And you will as well."

He hands the tops to Kim and Tim.

"You must have it on when you are at the camp," he adds.

Tim and Kim slip into the red tops. But they do not fit well. They are so big.

"I can swim in this," Kim grunts. "Is this for kids?"

Just then, there is a honk in front of the cabin.

"I do not expect a visit," says Mr. Prill. "Who can it be?"

He steps out.

Tim and Kim go out as well.

Can it be a kid who will be at this camp with them?

But there is no kid.

Chapter 5

A Visit From The Bank

There is a black BMW in front of the hut. A man with a black hat gets out with a grin. His hands are in his pockets.

"Well, Mr. Prill," the man says. "The bank sent me to ask if you have the rest of the funds. You got the cash yet?"

Mr. Prill grunts. "Mr. Vess, I just sent a big check to the bank. There must be a mix-up. I still have six days to get the rest."

"Just quit, will you," Mr. Vess snaps. "You got to admit it. You do not have the funds to pay the bank."

He steps in front of Mr. Prill.

"Did you not tell me that you were to set up a big camp with lots of kids to help you get a lump sum of cash?"

"We got kids in the camp," Mr. Prill says.

"Yes, I spot these next to you," Mr. Vess says. "But is that all? Where are the rest of the kids?"

He lifts his fist up.

"Did you expect this plan to get you out of this mess so quick? Did the ads for your camp get lost?" he says with a slick grin.

Mr. Prill gets all red.

"What did you do with my ads?" he blasts.

"Not a thing," Mr. Vess still grins. "Well, I will be back in six days. I bet you will not have the cash by then. We will evict you from the camp. And the bank will sell me this land."

Mr. Vess gets in his BMW and sets off fast.

Tim asks, "Does that man want this land?"

"Yes," Mr. Prill nods. He pats Tim on his back. "But do not think of all that, kids. You are at this camp to dig for fossils and have fun!"

Chapter 6
Mr. Prill's Granddad

They step back into the hut.

Mr. Prill brings out a pick from the cabinet.

"Is that a pickax?" Tim grins. "Is that for us? Do we get to hack things with it?"

His dad does not let Tim help with a pickax. This camp may not be as bad as he thinks.

"Yes, in fact, it is for you," Mr. Prill says. "But this is not a plaything. You cannot just slash things with it!"

Mr. Prill asks Tim to hand him the bucket. Tim grabs it from the top shelf. But the bucket slips and drops on a chest. The chest falls down and lands with a thud. A bunch of stuff spills out.

"Oh, no!" Tim gasps.

"That is O.K.," Mr. Prill says. "There are no fossils in there. That is all my granddad's junk."

Tim bends down to pick up the things. There is a lot of odd stuff that fell out of the chest.

"This is just trash that I must get rid of. I forgot they were still in there," Mr. Prill adds.

He picks up a hand lens with lots of dust and sets it on his desk.

"This is just a bunch of rubbish that rots in this chest. I will pack this up and drop it in the trash bin," he hums to himself.

He picks up a red hat and a red top from the chest.

"It still smells like my granddad," he says. "He was the best. He got this land. Then he set up this big log cabin as his ranch."

Mr. Prill dumps all of the stuff back in the chest.

"He was glad to get this ranch," Mr. Prill tells the kids. "All went well until he hit a fossil when he was digging to plant crops."

The kids can tell that Mr. Prill is sad.

"He felt that fossils were his calling," Mr. Prill adds. "He got rid of all his ranch hands and quit planting crops.

He shut down the ranch. Then, he set up a camp for digging fossils."

Kim picks up a small tin lockbox with lots of red rust spots.

"What is this black box?" she asks.

"Oh, that," Mr. Prill shrugs. "That was my granddad's as well."

Kim hands it back to Mr. Prill.

"But then he went nuts," he adds. "He went on and on telling odd things like he went back to the past. That he met a T-Rex. Just odd things like that."

Mr. Prill puffs the dust off the black box.

"He set up this box in his shed. He pled that it held the lock to the past and its link to our day." Mr. Prill dumps the box back in the chest with the rest.

"In the end, they had to lock him up in a clinic."

"That is so sad," Tim says.

"Yes, it is," nods Mr. Prill. "But that is not the topic of the day. Let us prep for the dig."

Chapter 7
The Fact Test

Mr. Prill claps his hands. "Set for a quiz? Can you tell me what a fossil is?"

"A fossil is a rock," Kim jumps in. "Or a fossil can be in a rock."

"Yes, in fact," Mr. Prill nods.

He steps next to the shelf and picks up a skull. "How do we get a fossil?"

"The skin and the flesh rot in the mud or the sand. And the rest is stuck in a rock," says Tim. "And that gets to be the fossil."

"Yes, that is it in a nutshell. I can tell you dug for facts to prep," grins Mr. Prill.

He hands the skull to Tim. "This is just a cast, not the fossil we dug out. But still, do not drop it."

Kim checks out the shells on Mr. Prill's shelf. There is a rock with a plant imprint next to the shells.

Mr. Prill says, "A fossil can be an imprint as well. They can tell us a lot."

"May I?" Kim asks.

"Go for it," says Mr. Prill.

He hands Kim the rock with a print of a plant.

Mr. Prill asks, "Can you think of things fossils can tell us?"

Tim lists his facts. "A print of a step can tell us how big a thing was. It can tell us how fast it ran when it was living."

"Yes, Tim," Mr. Prill says.

"And what its skin was like as well," Tim adds.

"They can tell what it was like on this planet back then," Mr. Prill tells the kids. "They are the best hints to our planet's past. That is why we do what we do at this camp."

He sits at his desk.

"I like the T-Rex. Which do you think is the best?" he asks.

"T-Rex," Tim and Kim lift their fists as they yell. "The king of the past!"

Mr. Prill grins. "The last quiz! Why did the T-Rex and the rest get extinct?"

"I think a comet hit our planet," says Kim. "It flung up so much dust that the dust did block out the sun. And that was the end for them."

"Well, you did well on the fact test. I can tell you are all set for this dig," Mr. Prill pats Kim on the back.

Then he brings out a small backpack with a strap.

"Just a last thing to discuss."

Mr. Prill hands Tim the backpack.

"Next step is to go out to the plots. This is not a dig in a sandbox. The things you will have with you are not just for fun. I expect top skills from you when you are out in the plot. Got it?"

Chapter 8
Prep For The Dig

Tim unzips the backpack. It has a brush, rags, flasks, sunblock and big red hats in it. He sets the backpack next to the bucket and the pick.

"Bring all this stuff with you to the digging plot," says Mr. Prill. "The pick is to dig with. If you have luck and spot a fossil, the brush is to get rid of the dust and the sand. If there is mud on it, you can rub it off with the rags."

Mr. Prill hands the flasks to Kim. "You can fill the flasks in the sink next to my bed. It gets hot out there. You must have lots to drink with you."

Kim fills the flasks from the tap and sets them next to the desk.

"Last, hats and sunblock," Mr. Prill adds. "You do not want to be in the sun all day with no hat or sunblock. Trust me on that."

He straps the hats on the kids.

Then he says, "Let me tell you the plan for the dig. This is the list of things to do: Do not rush! That is the list!" he slams his hand on his desk. "That is it!"

Kim and Tim flinch at the bang.

"It is how well you do the job at hand, not how quick you are," he adds.

The kids nod.

"If you crush a fossil, it will be trash. You cannot fix it. You cannot bring it back. Do not forget. Fossils are all we have left from the past," he tells them.

Kim and Tim get that this is a big job. They will not mess it up.

Tim lifts up the backpack and the pick. Kim picks up the bucket.

"You are all set. Let us go to your plot," says Mr. Prill as they exit his hut.

Chapter 9
The Plots

As they go up to the plot, Kim thinks of Mr. Vess.

"Is it just bad luck that the ads for the kids got lost?" Kim asks Mr. Prill. "Or do you think Mr. Vess had a hand in it?"

Mr. Prill grunts. "Mr. Vess is just up to his old tricks. But that is not for you kids to think of."

They stop in front of a mud pond.

"This is the plot!" He stabs a stick in the mud. "And this is where you dig."

The plot has red flags stuck onto pegs.

The kids stand still in shock. This is a dump!

"Can we dig in the next plot?" Tim asks. "This has so much mud."

"No, this is your plot," says Mr. Prill. "Get on with the dig. I must go back and finish up my stuff. I will be back to check on you."

"But the mud!" says Kim.

"The mud will not sting you! It is from the well. There is a crack in it. I did not fix it yet." Mr. Prill picks up the sticks and sets off back to his hut.

Kim and Tim are not glad to be stuck in this mud plot in the hot sun.

"This is no fun. We are stuck in this mess. Who wants to dig in the mud?"

she rants. "I wish we were back with Mom, Dad and Bud."

She drops the bucket.

"If this is Mr. Prill's plan for the kids' camp, it will be a flop," she adds. "I bet Mr. Vess and the bank will get the land."

"I wish we were with Mom and Dad as well. But let us have fun with what we got," Tim says.

He grabs the pick and digs in the mud.

Chapter 10
The Chest With The Junk

Kim and Tim dig and dig in the hot sun. Yet the stuff they dig out just slips back into the pit. It fills back up with mud fast.

"We cannot dig in the mud like this," yells Kim.

Mud drips down from her hands.

"I must have a drink," Tim says.

He rubs his hands on his pants to get rid of the mud. Then he checks the backpack.

"Where are the drinks?" he asks.

There are no flasks in the backpack.

"I set them in the backpack," Kim says. "Did I not?"

She checks the bag. But there are no drinks.

"I must have left them by the desk back at Mr. Prill's hut," she says.

"I will get them," grunts Tim.

"I will go with you," Kim says. "I must get a rest from this mud."

The kids go back to the hut. On the front steps, they spot the flasks. Next to the flasks is the chest with Mr. Prill's granddad's junk.

Tim swigs the drink in big gulps. It is still fresh. Then he sits down to rest next to the chest.

Kim sits on the steps and gets a quick sip from the flask.

Tim inspects the stuff in the chest.

"Mr. Prill may get mad at you if you prod at his chest," Kim says.

"I do not think so," says Tim. "He does not want this stuff. He plans to get rid of it. The chest is on its way to the trash."

Tim lifts things out of the chest.

"I think it is sad that Mr. Prill wants to dump this stuff," Tim says. "I just want to check out that black box."

Chapter 11
The Black Box

Tim digs out the box from the chest.

There is no lock on it. He wants to lift up the lid to check what is in it. But the lid is stuck. He grabs a rock and taps the top. The lid pops up.

There is a set of pins in the box.

The red pin says: BACK TO THE PAST.

The black pin says: BACK TO THE PRESENT.

On top of the pins, there is a switch. The 3-inch black display is blank.

"I want to check it out," Kim jumps up. "Let me have it!"

She grabs the box.

"Are these the on and off pins?" she asks.

The box slips out from her hand and drops in the sand. It lands flat on the pins with a bang.

There is a...

Tick.

Tick.

Tick.

"What is that?" asks Tim.

He picks up the black box fast. The display blinks BLAST OFF in red.

Then, a gust of wind picks up. Their hats drift in the wind.

Tim wants to press a pin to stop the blinking. But there is no pin that says on or off.

Then the lid of the box slams shut with a clang. It is as if a spell was cast.

The twisting wind sucks Kim, Tim and the black box up.

Did they just get into a big mess?

Chapter 12
Back To The Past

Kim and Tim vanish into the twisting wind. They yell at the top of their lungs to call for help.

They spin and spin until the wind kicks them out. They fall on their backs on the grass. The black box falls next to Tim with a thud.

The kids get up.

"What was that?" asks Kim in a panic. "Where did we end up? Where are we?"

Tim is in a shock as well. He picks up the black box.

"It must have hit the pin when you let the box drop," he says.

"Um, Tim," says Kim. She grabs his hand. "Where are the log cabin and Mr. Prill's hut?"

The kids stand in a tract of land with no end.

There is no cabin.

No hut or stalls.

No plots with strings and flags.

Just the land, the hills and cliffs that are all intact, as if no man was there.

It is melting hot as well. How did it get so hot so fast?

Tim still has the black box in his hand. Was it the box that got them there?

"The wind! I think the wind sent us to where we are," says Tim.

He lifts the lid to check if the box is still intact. The pins and the switch are still there. There is no crack on the display. It is just black and blank.

Tim wants to set off the black box and bring back the twisting wind. Yet he has no plan how to do it. There is no text that tells him what to do with the pins.

But then, there is a blink on the display.

It says: NEXT BLAST OFF IMPENDING.

Impending?

Tim hits the pins in a panic.

Click! Click! Click!

There is no tick.

No wind.

No gust.

Not a thing.

Can the box bring them back to where they were? Will it still do the job?

Chapter 13

The Duckbill's Nest

"I... I... I think we are where we were digging. But I think we went back to the past," Tim says.

"To the past?" Kim flips out. "Past where? How will we get back to Mom and Dad?"

Kim is so upset that she does not pick up on the big thuds. But Tim does.

"Uh, oh!" he gasps.

Steps from where they are, a big T-Rex stomps its legs. It twists and bends its big neck. It slaps the trunk of a sapling. A branch and a chunk of the sapling fall with a crash.

"Mad T-Rex!" Tim yells. "Run, Kim! Run!"

Tim spots a hill. He tells Kim to run to get out of the T-Rex's way. Then he directs her to the hill. They dash to the top.

When they get to the top, Tim yells, "Kim! Stop!"

Kim does not spot the nest in front of her. She trips and falls into the nest with a thump. She lands in the midst of a bunch of big eggs.

A big Duckbill stomps up to the nest with big grunts.

Kim sits up as Tim runs to the nest.

"Get out of there quick!" Tim pants. "We do not want the Duckbill Mom to spot us!"

Kim wants to get out of the nest. But her leg is stuck. She yanks her leg. But she falls down on her back.

Tim is frantic. In a panic, he drops the black box into the nest. He lifts the egg a bit and tugs Kim's leg out. Then he grabs her and helps her out of the nest.

"Why were you in my nest? Did you crack my eggs?" blasts the Duckbill.

She bends into the nest to check her eggs.

"Uh... I... You can chat?" Tim gasps in shock.

Chapter 14
The Missing Egg

"Yes, I can," yells the Duckbill. "Tell me. Why were you in my nest?"

"I fell in," says Kim. "Mad T-Rex. We ran off. I did not…"

"I am Tim. This is Kim," Tim jumps in. "We do not want to bug you. We just want to get out of your way."

"Did you crack my eggs?" The Duckbill Mom taps her eggs to check if there is a crack.

"No! No! No!" says Kim in a rush.

The Duckbill nods.

"All six eggs are O.K.," she says. "I am not mad. But I still do not want you back in my nest with my eggs."

The kids nod, still in shock.

The Duckbill says, "My eggs must be kept hot. I will get plants to set on top of them."

She pads the eggs with the twigs in the nest.

"Stay out of my nest," the Duckbill tells the kids.

Then she stomps off.

"I am so glad they did not crack!" Tim says. "You fell with such a big thud."

He checks the eggs.

"Did the Duckbill say she has six eggs in the nest?" he yelps.

"Yes," Kim nods.

"1 – 2 – 3 – 4 – 5. Then an egg is missing!" Tim gasps. "Where is the sixth egg?"

"I bet it fell out of the nest!" Kim says.

She spots the egg down the hill.

"No!" she yells. "It is next to that mad T-Rex!"

Chapter 15
The Mad T-Rex

"Oh, no!" Tim gasps.

"We must get that egg back to the nest!" Kim blasts.

"But the T-Rex?" Tim yelps in a panic.

The T-Rex still jumps up and down. It runs from shrub to shrub. It swings the branch it has in its hand and bangs it on the rocks.

"Yes, the T-Rex!" says Kim. "It will smash the egg if we do not get to it fast!"

"Or it will crush us when we get there," Tim grunts.

"But we cannot let the egg just sit there," Kim says.

"I will get the egg," Tim huffs.

He is not glad to do this task.

"Not just you," says Kim. "That is a big egg. I will help as well."

Tim nods. He thinks back to their last trip at Camp Split Rock. Kim was such a big help with the fox and the pet scam.

Plus, there was that trip where they met Sam, the Cod Fish, and Gup, the Ray Fish. Thanks to Kim's grand plan, they got Sam the Cod Fish out from the rocks where he was stuck.

Kim can be a big help with the T-Rex as well.

When the T-Rex runs to the left, the kids sprint down the hill.

As they run down, Tim steps on a plastic like thing and slips. He checks what it is.

"Yuck," he yells. "It is the Duckbill's shed skin."

The kids are down the hill. By then, the T-Rex is back as well. The egg sits on a bump next to a rock where the T-Rex is.

The kids stand still in shock. They think that the T-Rex may just gulp them down.

Then the T-Rex hits a branch with its neck. The branch splits and its neck gets stuck in it. It yells and twists but it cannot get out.

"Quick!" Kim yells. "Run to the egg. The T-Rex is stuck!"

Chapter 16
The Big Help

Tim runs and clasps the egg. But it is so big. He cannot pick it up at all.

The T-Rex sobs and yells.

Tim just stops and stands still. He thinks its yells may just be for help.

"Tim!" yells Kim. "Do not just stand there. Get back! Quick!"

Tim says, "I do not think this T-Rex is bad. I think it just wants our help."

"Help?" Kim says. "Help with what? To crush us into dust?"

"No," says Tim. "Check out its gum. A big twig is stuck in there!"

The T-Rex stops yelling. It nods at Tim as it sobs.

"I think it gets what I say!" says Tim. "Just like that Duckbill."

"If there is a twig stuck in its gum, it will not be me who gets it out," says Kim.

The T-Rex twists his neck but it is still stuck. Tim is like a speck next to this big T-Rex.

"What if it is a trick?" Kim adds.

"Trick for what?" asks Tim.

"What got into you, Tim?" Kim blasts. "A trick so it can gulp us down! We can be its next lunch."

"I do not think it is a trick," says Tim.

He steps on a big rock so he is as tall as the T-Rex's neck.

"Um, Mr. T-Rex," he says in a timid way. "I think you have a twig stuck in your gum. Is that so?"

The T-Rex grunts and nods.

"I will help you with the branch and the twig," says Tim. "But no tricks!"

The T-Rex nods.

Tim gets its neck out of the branch. Then he yanks the twig but it is stuck.

"Ow!" the T-Rex yells.

Tim panics and falls down from the rock.

"I did not want to panic you," the T-Rex sniffs. "But my gum stings. I cannot help but yell."

Tim gets back on the rock. He will not stop until the twig is out. He grabs the twig and tugs it off. It pops out of the T-Rex's gum.

The T-Rex spits out the twig and rubs its gum with a grin.

"At last!" it says. "Thanks so much. You were such a big help. That twig was stuck in my gum for days!"

"I am glad to help," Tim grins.

Chapter 17

Man With The Black Box

Kim sprints to Tim.

"You are like that man that I met," the T-Rex says. "I wish he was back."

"What man?" Kim asks in shock.

The T-Rex says, "The man with the box."

"Did you say a box?" Tim yelps. "Was it a black box?"

"Yes, he had a black box," says the T-Rex.

"Is that who I think it is?" Kim gasps.

"Where did that man go?" asks Tim.

"He left. Puff. Just like that. He went off with a twisting wind."

"So Mr. Prill's granddad did visit the past! And he went back. Then the box can bring us back as well!" the kids yell as they jump up and down.

"Let us check the box," Kim says with a shrill.

But Tim and Kim cannot spot the black box.

"Where can it be, Tim? That is our way back." Kim is on a hunt for the box.

"I think I left it up the hill by the nest. We must get up and check there," Tim tells Kim. "Plus, we must bring the egg back to the nest."

The egg is big. Tim and Kim cannot bring it up the hill back to the nest.

"I can help," the T-Rex jumps in. "If you let me."

Tim and Kim nod.

The T-Rex picks up the egg. The kids and the T-Rex run up the hill back to the nest. They pop the missing egg back in.

Tim checks the nest. The black box is in there. Its lid is up.

He brings the box out. The display is still blank.

"What is up with this box?" he grunts. "Why is the display all black?"

The pins are there. But the switch is missing.

"It must be the switch," he yelps. "Where is it?"

"It may still be in the nest," says Kim. "Check in there!"

Tim jumps back in with the eggs. He digs in the twigs. Then he jumps up with a big grin.

"I got it! I got it!" He has the switch in his hand.

Tim jumps out of the nest in a rush just as the Duckbill gets back with lots of plants. He does not want her to spot him in the nest.

He sticks the switch back in. The display blinks.

Then it says: NEXT BLAST OFF IS T.B.D.

"I think the box is back on," Tim jumps up.

Chapter 18

A Trip On T-Rex's Back

The Duckbill gets back. She dumps the plants on top of the nest. "I got a hunch. I think this is the day my eggs will crack."

"They will?" gasps Kim. "I want to be back with Mom and Dad. But I do not want to miss the eggs cracking!"

"We may still have to stay for just a bit until it says BLAST OFF," Tim tells Kim.

Kim is glad that they can go back and still not miss the eggs cracking.

"Can we stay with you by the nest?" Kim asks the Duckbill.

The Duckbill nods.

They sit next to the nest.

"I wish to bring back an egg with me," Kim thinks. But she does not say a thing. She can tell the Duckbill Mom will not like that.

"When will they crack?" Kim asks.

Tim says, "Duckbill eggs have thick shells."

He thinks of the experiment with the eggs in his class. At the end, small chicks got out of the eggs.

This tops that hands down.

Then he adds, "I bet this will not be as quick as you wish."

"What can we do? I do not want to sit still by the nest," Kim says with a shrug.

"If you are up for a quick trip, I can bring you to the best spot to check out our land," the T-Rex says. "It will be a trip you will not forget."

"Yes! Yes! Yes!" The kids jump up and down.

"Hop on my back," winks the T-Rex.

"But I do not want to miss the eggs cracking," says Kim.

"How quick can you be?" Tim asks the T-Rex.

"As quick as you want me to be! I can get you there fast. We can be back by the nest when the eggs crack," the T-Rex says.

The Duckbill Mom tends to her eggs as the kids jump on the T-Rex's back.

The T-Rex runs as fast as the wind, crushing the plants as it steps on them.

The kids hang on to the big bumps on its neck so they do not fall down. Its skin is thick.

As they pass by, the kids spot a pack of T-Rex that hangs out on the grass.

The T-Rex stops at a big rock by a cliff. Tim and Kim hop down.

It nods to its left. "That is the best spot of all this land."

The kids go to the left and stand at the tip of the cliff.

There it is in front of them. The setting is enchanting. A blanket of bliss spans the land. It is just stunning.

"Just hop back on when you are set to go," the T-Rex says.

"I do not want to go back just yet," Kim grunts.

"We must be quick if you want to be there when the eggs crack," Tim tells Kim.

The eggs!

She forgot the eggs!

They hop back on the T-Rex. They sprint to the nest in a flash.

Chapter 19
The Eggs Crack

When they are back at the nest, Tim checks the black box.

The display says: NEXT BLAST OFF AT WILL.

"Yes!" he says. "We can go back when we wish."

Kim runs to the eggs. An egg shifts a bit. At last, it cracks. Then the next, and the next.

Small duckbills get out of the shells bit by bit. They are wet as if they just got back from a swim in a pond.

This stuns Kim.

This is not just a quest.

This is a thrill.

Kim plays with the nestlings as Tim gets up to check the black box.

The display still says: NEXT BLAST OFF AT WILL.

Plus, it blinks.

Tim gets up quick.

"Kim, the display is blinking. We must go," he says. "We cannot risk it. I do not want to be stuck in the past."

Kim gets up fast.

It is fun to be with the Duckbill Mom, the nestlings and the T-Rex. But she does not want to miss the trip back to the present.

"Tim," she says. "What if we bring fossils from the past with us? That may help Mr. Prill with the bank."

"These are not fossils yet, Kim." Tim hints that this will not do the trick with the bank.

Kim jumps in, "What if we bring the fresh stuff with us? We can ask the Duckbill for the eggshells."

"Yes!" Tim grins. "The merits of fresh Duckbill eggshells will top the fossils. It can help Mr. Prill fund the camp and pay back the bank. Then he can stop that Mr. Vess."

Chapter 20

The Twisting Wind Is Back

Kim thinks of the shed skin where Tim slid down the hill. She runs to pick that up as well.

She asks the Duckbill if they can bring back a bit of the eggshells and the shed skin with them.

"The eggshells and the shed skin?" the Duckbill asks. "Why do you want them? They are just trash!"

"Where we are from, they are not trash at all," Kim says.

The Duckbill shrugs. "You are such odd things. But if it helps you, why not?"

"Thank you so much!" Tim says with a big grin.

"We wish you and the nestlings well. But we must go back," Kim says.

"Be well," says the Duckbill.

The kids fill their pockets to the brim with all they can get their hands on.

"I had a hunch that you will not stay with us," says the T-Rex.

Tim nods.

"We want to be back with Mom and Dad. But we will miss you," Tim says.

The T-Rex bends down and squints.

Then it asks Tim, "Is it a fact that we will be extinct? That man did say that there was not a T-Rex left where he was from."

Tim pats the T-Rex. He can tell it is sad.

"Yes, but do not let that get you down," he says. "You are still the king of this land."

"Thank you for the help with the twig," T-Rex says with half a grin. "I will miss you."

"Thank you for your help with the egg." Tim hugs its big leg. "We will miss you as well."

He lifts the lid of the black box.

Kim nods at Tim. "You can press the pin, Tim. I am all set."

Chapter 21
Back To The Present

Tim grabs Kim's hand.

Then he hits the black pin.

Tick.

Tick.

Tick.

The wind picks up. Then it spins into a twisting wind.

Tim still has the black box in his hand.

The kids jump in the wind. It spins them and then spits them out on its back end. They land on Mr. Prill's steps with a thud. They end up next to the chest with all the junk.

They spot the log cabin and the flag with the T-Rex print. Stacks of hay are still in the stalls. The plots with digs and pits are all there in front of them.

The kids are back at camp.

Just then, Mr. Prill steps out.

"There you are," he says. "Are you checking the junk in my granddad's chest?"

"Yes," says Tim with a grin. "This black box."

"That box is just crap," shrugs Mr. Prill.

"Do not be so fast to get rid of it," Tim says. "Your granddad held the link to the past. It was this box. This is the link!"

"He was not nuts. He went back to the past. He met a T-Rex," Kim jumps in. "We met that T-Rex as well."

"Uh, oh!" Mr. Prill drops down on the steps. "What got into you, kids? How will I tell your mom and dad that you went nuts? They will kill me!"

Chapter 22
A Gift For Mr. Prill

The kids have big grins.

Tim nods at Kim. Then he drops the black box into the chest.

They bring out all the things in their pockets.

"Check out what we got!" they yell.

They set down the Duckbill eggshells and the shed skin on the steps in front of Mr. Prill.

"Is this what I think it is?" Mr. Prill gasps in shock. "Where did you get this stuff from? How did you get your hands on all these?"

"Well," says Kim, "we went back to the past just like your granddad, thanks to his black box."

"What do you think of this stuff we got?" asks Tim. "Can this help you get Mr. Vess off your back? Will this bring in lots of cash so you can pay the bank?"

"I say yes!" yells Mr. Prill with a shrill. "Oh, kids! You are the best. Thanks to you, I will not go bankrupt. Thank you so much!"

He claps his hands.

"Quick! I got six days left to pay the bank back. I must call my pals. I will ask them to check out this stuff. Then I can sell all these to get the cash." Then he adds, "The black box is yours if you want it!"

Tim and Kim yell, "Yes! Yes! Yes!"

Mr. Prill runs into his hut with a skip in his step.

"This was the best present to bring to the present!" Kim winks.

Tim picks the black box up from the chest.

"So how can we tell Mom and Dad what this box can do?" Tim asks Kim with a wink.

The kids did not expect all this from Camp Diggin.

This was still the best quest of all... yet!

You can download full color

CERTIFICATE OF ACCOMPLISHMENT
and
CERTIFICATE OF COMPLETION

on our website

SIMPLEWORDSBOOKS.COM

Certificate of Accomplishment

This certificate is awarded to

_____

for successful completion of

Back To The Past

_____   _____
Signature   Date

BACK TO THE PAST

WORD LIST

You can download the full
word list on our website

simplewordsbooks.com

#	Word	Count	#	Word	Count	#	Word	Count
1	a	193	27	bench	1	53	bud	9
2	adds	15	28	bends	4	54	bug	1
3	admit	1	29	best	10	55	bump	1
4	ads	4	30	bet	5	56	bumps	1
5	all	32	31	big	38	57	bunch	3
6	am	6	32	bin	1	58	bus	6
7	an	4	33	bit	7	59	but	47
8	and	143	34	black	32	60	by	11
9	are	55	35	blank	3	61	cabin	9
10	as	46	36	blanket	1	62	cabinet	1
11	ask	5	37	blast	7	63	call	3
12	asks	27	38	blasts	4	64	calling	1
13	at	39	39	blink	1	65	camp	43
14	back	72	40	blinking	2	66	can	54
15	backpack	8	41	blinks	3	67	cannot	15
16	backs	1	42	bliss	1	68	cash	6
17	backup	1	43	block	1	69	cast	2
18	bad	6	44	BMW	2	70	chat	1
19	bag	1	45	box	47	71	check	18
20	bags	1	46	branch	7	72	checking	1
21	bang	2	47	brim	1	73	checks	7
22	bangs	1	48	bring	16	74	chest	18
23	bank	11	49	brings	4	75	chicks	1
24	bankrupt	1	50	brunch	1	76	chop	2
25	be	54	51	brush	2	77	chunk	1
26	bed	2	52	bucket	5	78	clang	1

#	Word	Count
79	claps	3
80	clasps	1
81	class	1
82	click	3
83	cliff	2
84	cliffs	1
85	clinic	1
86	cod	2
87	comet	1
88	contact	1
89	contracts	1
90	cops	1
91	crack	10
92	cracking	3
93	cracks	1
94	crap	1
95	crash	1
96	crops	2
97	crush	3
98	crushing	1
99	cub	1
100	dad	18
101	damp	1
102	dash	1
103	day	8
104	days	9

#	Word	Count
105	desk	8
106	did	26
107	dig	20
108	Diggin	12
109	digging	8
110	digs	4
111	directs	1
112	discuss	1
113	display	10
114	do	50
115	does	14
116	down	26
117	drag	1
118	dress	1
119	drift	1
120	drink	3
121	drinks	2
122	drips	1
123	drop	3
124	drops	6
125	Duckbill	26
126	duckbills	1
127	dug	2
128	dump	2
129	dumps	3
130	dust	7

#	Word	Count
131	egg	19
132	eggs	25
133	eggshells	5
134	enchanting	1
135	end	8
136	epic	1
137	evict	1
138	exit	1
139	expect	4
140	expects	1
141	experiment	1
142	extinct	2
143	fact	5
144	facts	2
145	fall	9
146	falls	5
147	fast	11
148	fell	4
149	felt	1
150	fill	2
151	fills	2
152	finish	1
153	fish	3
154	fist	1
155	fists	1
156	fit	1

#	Word	Count
157	fix	2
158	flag	3
159	flags	2
160	flaps	1
161	flash	1
162	flask	1
163	flasks	7
164	flat	2
165	flesh	1
166	flinch	1
167	flips	1
168	flop	1
169	flung	1
170	flush	1
171	for	44
172	forget	2
173	forgot	2
174	fossil	11
175	fossils	16
176	fox	2
177	frantic	1
178	fresh	4
179	from	24
180	front	12
181	fun	13
182	fund	1

#	Word	Count
183	funds	2
184	gasps	8
185	get	49
186	gets	17
187	glad	8
188	go	29
189	got	24
190	grabs	9
191	grand	1
192	granddad	8
193	grass	2
194	grin	8
195	grins	8
196	grunts	10
197	gulp	2
198	gulps	1
199	gum	7
200	Gup	1
201	gust	2
202	hack	1
203	had	6
204	half	1
205	hand	13
206	hands	17
207	hang	2
208	hangs	1

#	Word	Count
209	has	12
210	hat	3
211	hats	4
212	have	27
213	hay	2
214	he	124
215	held	2
216	help	22
217	helps	3
218	her	19
219	hill	9
220	hills	1
221	him	9
222	himself	1
223	hints	2
224	his	37
225	hit	3
226	hits	3
227	honk	1
228	hop	4
229	hot	7
230	how	12
231	huffs	1
232	hugs	1
233	hums	1
234	hunch	2

#	Word	Count	#	Word	Count	#	Word	Count
235	hunt	1	261	kid	2	287	lots	11
236	hut	16	262	kids	57	288	luck	3
237	I	100	263	kill	1	289	lump	1
238	if	28	264	Kim	126	290	lunch	1
239	impending	2	265	king	2	291	lungs	1
240	imprint	2	266	land	11	292	mad	5
241	in	121	267	lands	3	293	man	12
242	inch	1	268	last	9	294	mascot	2
243	ink	1	269	left	12	295	may	12
244	inn	2	270	leg	4	296	me	14
245	insists	1	271	legs	1	297	melting	1
246	inspects	1	272	lens	1	298	merits	1
247	intact	2	273	let	13	299	mess	6
248	into	15	274	lid	7	300	met	5
249	is	161	275	lift	2	301	midst	1
250	it	139	276	lifts	8	302	miss	7
251	its	20	277	like	21	303	missing	3
252	job	3	278	link	3	304	mix-up	1
253	jump	6	279	list	2	305	mock-up	1
254	jumps	11	280	lists	1	306	mom	22
255	junk	4	281	living	1	307	Mr.	89
256	just	52	282	lock	3	308	Mrs.	6
257	Kent	9	283	lockbox	1	309	much	6
258	Kents	1	284	log	5	310	mud	16
259	kept	1	285	lost	2	311	must	21
260	kicks	1	286	lot	5	312	my	23

#	Word	Count	#	Word	Count	#	Word	Count
313	nags	1	339	pals	1	365	plaything	1
314	neck	7	340	panic	5	366	pled	1
315	nest	31	341	panics	1	367	plot	8
316	nestlings	3	342	pants	3	368	plots	5
317	next	28	343	pass	1	369	plus	5
318	no	34	344	past	16	370	pocket	1
319	nod	3	345	pats	4	371	pockets	3
320	nods	14	346	pay	4	372	pond	2
321	not	85	347	pegs	1	373	pop	1
322	nuts	3	348	pet	2	374	pops	2
323	nutshell	1	349	pets	1	375	prep	2
324	NYC	1	350	pick	9	376	present	4
325	O.K.	2	351	pickax	2	377	press	2
326	odd	5	352	picks	12	378	Prill	69
327	of	91	353	pin	7	379	print	5
328	off	20	354	pins	8	380	prod	1
329	oh	6	355	pit	1	381	puff	1
330	old	3	356	pits	2	382	puffs	1
331	on	67	357	plan	8	383	pup	4
332	onto	1	358	planet	3	384	pups	1
333	or	8	359	plans	1	385	quest	2
334	our	7	360	plant	3	386	quick	14
335	out	57	361	planting	1	387	quit	3
336	ow	1	362	plants	4	388	quiz	2
337	pack	3	363	plastic	1	389	rags	2
338	pads	1	364	plays	1	390	ran	2

#	Word	Count		#	Word	Count		#	Word	Count
391	ranch	5		417	says	88		443	skin	8
392	rants	1		418	scam	2		444	skip	1
393	ray	1		419	sell	2		445	skull	2
394	red	11		420	sent	4		446	skulls	1
395	rest	9		421	set	16		447	slams	2
396	rid	6		422	sets	5		448	slaps	1
397	risk	1		423	setting	1		449	slash	1
398	rock	14		424	she	34		450	slick	1
399	rocks	4		425	shed	6		451	slid	1
400	rot	1		426	shelf	4		452	slip	1
401	rots	1		427	shells	5		453	slips	4
402	rub	1		428	shifts	1		454	small	4
403	rubbish	1		429	shock	7		455	smash	1
404	rubs	2		430	shrill	2		456	smell	1
405	run	7		431	shrub	2		457	smells	1
406	run-down	1		432	shrug	2		458	snack	1
407	runs	10		433	shrugs	3		459	snaps	1
408	rush	3		434	shut	2		460	sniffs	1
409	rust	1		435	sink	1		461	so	24
410	rustic	1		436	sinks	1		462	sobs	2
411	sad	4		437	sip	1		463	spans	1
412	sam	2		438	sit	3		464	speck	1
413	sand	4		439	sits	5		465	spell	1
414	sandbox	1		440	six	9		466	spend	3
415	sapling	2		441	sixth	1		467	spills	1
416	say	8		442	skills	1		468	spin	2

#	Word	Count
469	spin	2
470	spins	2
471	spits	2
472	split	3
473	splits	1
474	spot	11
475	spots	3
476	spring	2
477	sprint	2
478	sprints	1
479	squints	2
480	stabs	1
481	stack	1
482	stacks	2
483	staff	3
484	stalls	4
485	stamps	1
486	stand	5
487	stands	2
488	stay	5
489	step	4
490	steps	13
491	stick	1
492	sticks	2
493	still	28
494	sting	1

#	Word	Count
495	stings	1
496	stomps	3
497	stop	5
498	stops	4
499	strap	1
500	straps	1
501	strict	1
502	strings	1
503	stuck	16
504	stuff	15
505	stunning	1
506	stuns	1
507	such	5
508	sucks	1
509	sum	1
510	sun	4
511	sunblock	3
512	swigs	1
513	swim	2
514	swings	1
515	switch	6
516	T.B.D.	1
517	tag	1
518	tall	2
519	tap	1
520	taps	2

#	Word	Count
521	task	1
522	tell	20
523	telling	1
524	tells	14
525	ten	1
526	tends	1
527	test	1
528	text	1
529	thank	4
530	thanks	4
531	that	84
532	the	553
533	their	13
534	them	27
535	then	36
536	there	56
537	these	5
538	they	70
539	thick	2
540	thing	7
541	things	11
542	think	26
543	thinks	11
544	this	82
545	thrill	1
546	thud	4

#	Word	Count
547	thump	1
548	tick	7
549	tickets	1
550	Tim	140
551	timid	1
552	tin	1
553	tip	1
554	to	190
555	top	13
556	topic	1
557	tops	4
558	track	1
559	tract	1
560	trash	6
561	T-Rex	63
562	trick	5
563	tricks	2
564	trip	12
565	trips	1
566	trunk	1
567	trust	1
568	tugs	2
569	twig	10
570	twigs	2
571	twisting	5
572	twists	3

#	Word	Count
573	uh	3
574	um	2
575	until	7
576	unzips	1
577	up	58
578	upset	1
579	us	22
580	vanish	1
581	Vess	11
582	visit	2
583	wall	1
584	want	28
585	wants	8
586	was	30
587	way	6
588	we	64
589	well	29
590	went	11
591	were	11
592	west	1
593	wet	1
594	what	34
595	when	17
596	where	24
597	which	1
598	who	7

#	Word	Count
599	why	7
600	will	75
601	wind	15
602	wink	1
603	winks	2
604	wish	8
605	with	106
606	yanks	2
607	yell	6
608	yelling	1
609	yells	13
610	yelps	4
611	yes	23
612	yet	8
613	you	119
614	your	11
615	yours	1
616	yuck	1
Total Words		**7209**

Do you want to write your own story now?

Written by:

_____

_____

_____

_____

_____

_____

_____

_____

_____

_____

_____

_____

_____

_____

_____

_____

_____

_____

_____

_____

_____

_____

_____

_____

Do you want to draw your own story now?

Illustrated by:

EARLY LEVEL CHAPTER BOOKS
www.simplewordsbooks.com

HIGHER LEVEL CHAPTER BOOKS

STUDY GUIDES

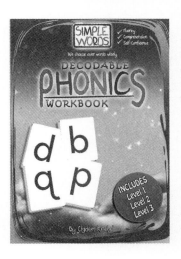